This Roary The
Racing Car Annual
2011 belongs to

....

First published in Great Britain by
HarperCollins Children's Books in 2010
1 3 5 7 9 10 8 6 4 2
ISBN: 978-0-00-736606-4

Based on the television series Roary the Racing Car
© Chapman Entertainment & David Jenkins 2010

Visit Roary at www.roarytheracingcar.com

Chapman
ENTERTAINMENT

Printed and bound in China

Annual 2011

STOP
RACECARS

HarperCollins *Children's Books*

Contents

1

Welcome to Silver Hatch

You're just in time for race day. How many of the pictures at the bottom of the page can you find in this big image?

a

b

c

8

d

e

f

Two Wheel Driver

Maxi hummed a little song as Big Chris topped up his oil. His engine had been tuned and he couldn't wait to get out on the track.

"It's a special day for you today, eh Maxi?" grinned Big Chris. "Not many cars get to star in Silver Hatch's Stunt Spectacular!"

Marsha checked Drifter's onboard computer then ticked her form.

"Looks like you're all set too." Drifter beamed. "Thank you, Marsha!" Big Chris opened the workshop doors then peered across to the grandstand. "The crowds are flocking in already," he whistled. "And there's Mr Carburettor, right on cue."

Big Chris waved the cars outside just as Mr Carburettor touched down in Hellie. "Mamma Mia!" he gasped, running over to greet them. "Is everything ready?" The racetrack boss pulled out a silk hankie and polished Cici's number 3. Silver Hatch's Stunt Spectacular was one of the biggest events of the year – everything had to be just right.

"The cars know their routines inside out," said Marsha.

Mr Carburettor nodded. "Good, good. I wanna see wheelies, high speed turns, all your best moves!"

"Morning all!" shouted PC Pete, walking across to say hello. "I'm here for a quick safety check."

"Cici's been practising her moves for months," piped up Roary. "She won't hurt herself!"

Big Chris patted Roary's bonnet. "You can never be too careful, lad. Anyway Maxi, Drifter and Tin Top are going to be out there too."

"What about me?" shouted Roary.

"I can do stunts!"

Big Chris shook his head. "I need you to keep all four wheels on the ground today."

"Stunts can be dangerous," added PC Pete. "You'll be able to join the team when you're older."

Roary pulled into a side bay so that the other cars could get in some last minute practice for the Stunt Spectacular show.

"I'm gonna wow the crowds with my basketball skills," grinned Tin Top, balancing a ball on his bumper. Drifter's headlights flickered as he booted up his computer.

"Wait till I turn on my rocket boosters!"

"Mine's the best stunt," announced Maxi. "I'm going to perform a high-speed race around the track... in reverse!"

As the cars took turns showing off their tricks, Cici couldn't help but notice how sad Roary looked.

"Don't worry," she whispered. "Next year you'll be ready to drive in the Spectacular too."

Roary's bumpers slumped sadly. "But I'm ready now!"

Cici glided into an elegant three point turn. "Wheelies and jumps are not as easy as they look!"

Just then, Marsha began signalling the team into the pit lane.

"Maxi! Tin Top! Drifter! Cici!" she called. "On track in five please."

"See you, Roary," shouted Maxi, skidding out onto the track.

3

When the other cards had zoomed out to the track, Roary reversed back into the workshop.

"Aren't you going to come and watch son?" asked Big Chris.

"Nah," sighed Roary. "I'm not in the mood for the Stunt Spectacular."

"Did someone say 'Stunt Spectacular'?" boomed an excited voice. "Watcha Roary!"

The little red racing car looked up to see Flash scoot in.

"I'll leave you two to it then," said Big Chris, heading off to the commentary tower.

Roary explained to Flash that he was too young for the stunt team.

"Nonsense!" scoffed the rabbit. "We need to show the crowd what you can do."

Flash led Roary out to the track, then ushered him into the pits.

"The team's big routine only lasts twenty minutes," he sniggered.

"When they come off, you can go on."

"Are you sure I won't get into trouble?" asked Roary. Flash shook his head.

"Big Chris will be knocked out when he sees your wild wheelies!"

Roary gulped nervously as Maxi started the show. The fans cheered as he expertly flipped his tyres up then swerved into a high speed reverse. A dozen newspaper reporters started snapping his picture.

"I'll weigh the end of my skateboard down with a rock," Flash told Roary. "Then you can use it as a ramp. They'll love it!"

When all the cars had finished their display, Silver Hatch echoed with applause.

"Don't go away folks!" commentated Big Chris. "We'll be back on track in five minutes."

"Your turn!" urged Flash. "The skateboard's all ready."

Roary revved his engine, then screeched onto the track. He skidded over the mini ramp and pulled his front wheels up as high as he could.

"Look! I'm doing a wheelie!" shouted Roary.

"Roary!" Big Chris leaned out of the commentary tower and gasped. "What's going on?"

Roary wheelied all the way up Hard Brake Hill. The other cars blinked and beeped their horns as he whizzed past at top speed.
"You're a sensation!" bellowed Flash, grabbing his board then following after.
"This is fun!" called Roary. "I've never gone this far on two... woah!"

Suddenly the racing car's tyres skidded on the tarmac. Roary tried to brake, but he was veering out of control.
"Help!" shouted Roary, as he wobbled and spun into the safety cones.
"Number one's landed in a pile of mud," announced Big Chris, switching off his microphone. "And a whole heap of trouble."

3

1

Roary's engine spluttered then stopped. The poor car was up to his wing mirrors in thick, squelchy mud.

"I think I went too fast, Flash," he sighed. "Flash?"

Roary looked left and right before catching sight of the naughty rabbit running back to his burrow.

Cici was on the scene in seconds.

"Are you alright?" she cried. "What were you doing out there?"

Roary shook his head in shame.

"I'm so sorry. I just wanted to do some stunts too."

"You should have checked with me first, lad!" Big Chris told him, motoring up in Plugger.

When they got back to the Workshop, Big Chris heard the full story.

"Look at the state of you!" he sighed, washing Roary's bodywork. "How you didn't have a nasty accident I'll never know."

Before Roary could say another word, the office phone began to ring. It was bound to be Marsha calling to say how cross Mr Carburettor was.

Big Chris chatted on the line for a minute, then slowly wandered back.

"You'd better fetch Flash," he said. "Apparently the crowd loved your appearance in the Stunt Spectacular."

"Wh-what?" stuttered Roary. Big Chris nodded. "They went nuts for the two wheel spin. You've been very lucky."

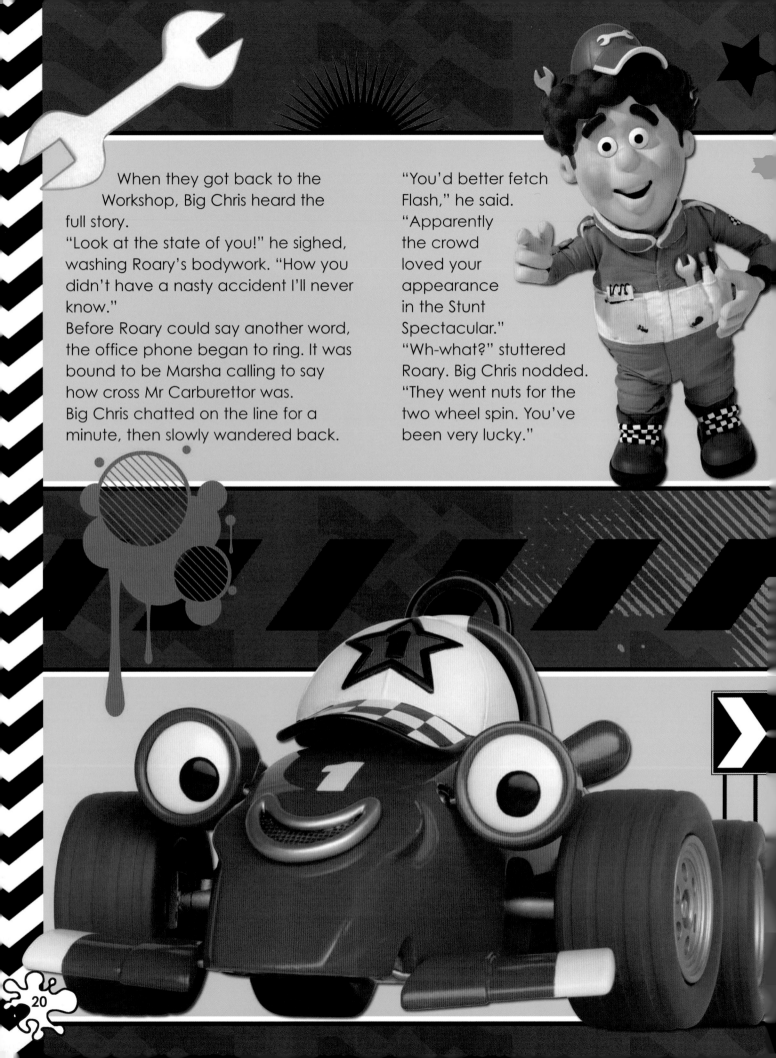

Roary and Flash slowly
made their way out to
meet the others.
"This was all my idea,"
said Flash sheepishly.
"I'm sorry everyone."
Roary dipped his
headlights at PC Pete.
"From now on I'll only try a
stunt if I get permission first."
The policeman patted Roary's
bonnet then smiled knowingly
at Marsha and Big Chris.
"That's the idea, Roary."

But as soon as the single-seater turned
onto the track, the grandstand erupted in
applause.
"Here's my little star!" beamed Mr
Carburettor, pushing his way past a
cluster of reporters.
Roary pulled up next to Maxi. "Does
he mean me?"
"For some reason your silly mud bath
stole the show," he sniffed.
"Time for a lap of honour," giggled Cici.
"Coming?"
Roary revved his engine. "You bet, but
from now on I'm sticking to four wheels!"

21

Puddle Paths

Roary wants to splash through as many puddles as possible on his way to see Drifter! Which path should he follow?

a

b

c

Draw Tin Top

Woah! Tin Top has crashed and his friends have to jump over him!
Draw poor Tin Top sitting on the track.

23

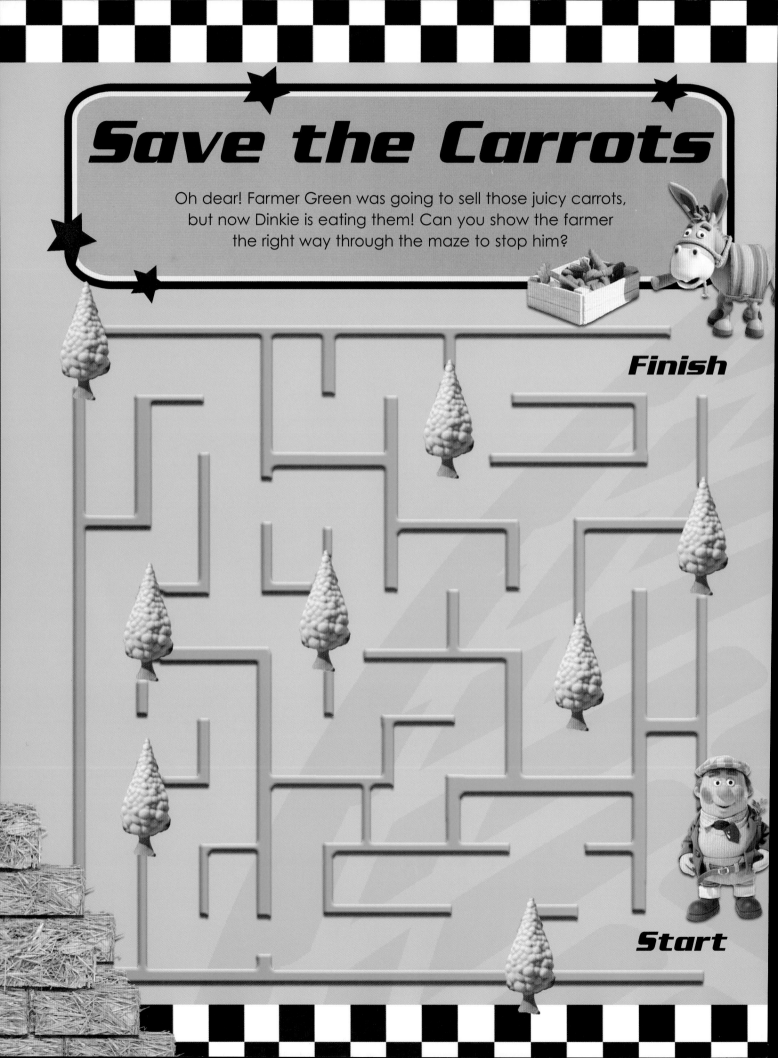

Save the Carrots

Oh dear! Farmer Green was going to sell those juicy carrots, but now Dinkie is eating them! Can you show the farmer the right way through the maze to stop him?

Finish

Start

Sing Along

Big Chris and his mum Big Christine are singing Roary's song!
Can you sing along with them? The words are printed below.

I love that car
My number one star
At the Silver Hatch
In his little white cap
Come on Roary, one more lap!

Roary the Racing Car
Roary the number one star
He's coming to the line
Looking real fine
Watch out Roary,
they're right behind you!

Ball Bounce

Whee! Breeze throws her beach ball up into the air.
Follow the lines to see who catches it.

Maxi

Breeze

Tin
Top

Roary

26

Lost Post

Big Chris got five letters this morning,
but they've blown away in the wind!
Can you find them all without waking Rusty up?

Match the Drivers

Can you draw lines to match the drivers to their favourite vehicles?

a

b

c

1   2   3

Colour Mr Carburettor

Oh dear, Mr Carburettor is annoyed with Flash again! What do you think he is saying? Colour him in, then write some words in the speech bubble.

29

Shadow Spotting

Can you guess who each of these characters are, just by looking at their shadows?

a

b

c

d

Jigsaw Jiggle

There's a piece missing from this picture of Flash and Molecom.
Can you work out which one it is?
Write your answer in the box below.

31

Restore Roary's Redness

Roary asked Molecom to give him a new coat of paint, and the short-sighted mole coloured him white! Use your crayons to make him red again.

Tidying-up Time

It's race day and Marsha is getting everything ready.
But there's a lot of mess to clear away first.
Circle the objects that aren't needed at the workshop.

Job Match

Can you draw lines to match the vehicles to the descriptions of the jobs they do?

Hellie

a He carries the cars on journeys to far-away places.

b He rescues broken-down cars.

Plugger

c He carries Mr Carburettor around.

Loada

Get Set, Join the Dots

Join the dots to help Maxi start the race!
Then colour him in with your brightest crayon.

1

Clever Chris!

Big Chris is juggling tools from the workshop to entertain the cars!
Can you count how many of each object he is juggling?

There are ☐ wrenches

There are ☐ spanners

There are ☐ screwdrivers

Draw Roary

Draw a picture of Roary in the grid, using the picture below as a guide.

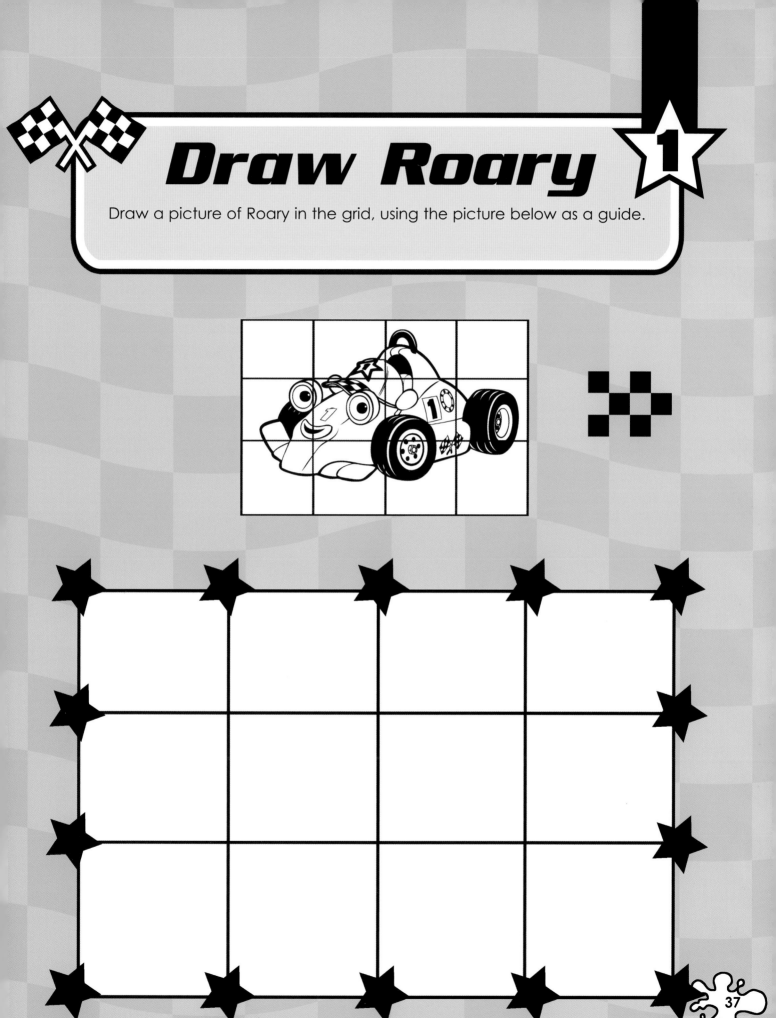

The Best Friends Ever

"Good morning, Silver Hatch!" yawned Big Chris, rubbing his eyes before stumbling down Rusty's steps. Rusty the caravan blinked and looked around him.
"It's a chilly one today."
"That's because it's nearly Christmas!" replied the mechanic. "I wonder if it'll snow?"
"In the good old days we always had lots of snow at this time of year," sighed Rusty. "Such fun..."
Big Chris clapped his hands and then chuckled. "It's gonna be a good one this year too, just you wait!"
While Rusty settled down for another forty winks, his friend headed straight out to the workshop.

Big Chris woke up Roary and his friends, then grabbed a morning cuppa.

"I need to zoom through my jobs today," he told them. "My mum's coming over tonight."

"Big Christine!" cheered Tin Top. "Is she going to stay for Christmas?"

The mechanic nodded. "Yep! The tree's got to be up and decorated before she arrives."

Roary beeped his horn. "We'll help you get ready, Big Chris!"

"Thank you Roary," he replied. "I want it to be the best Christmas ever!"

Just then, Marsha ran onto the forecourt. "Tea break's over, I'm afraid," she said, glancing at her clipboard. "I've got a heap of chores for you, Big Chris."

Big Chris's face fell as Marsha handed over a super-long list of jobs.
"Ah, Marsha, love," he argued. 'I'll never get through this lot today!"
Marsha sighed and shook her head. "I'm afraid you have to, Big Chris. Mr Carburettor wants this lot ticked off before Christmas."
As soon as Silver Hatch's Race Marshall had gone, Big Chris got cracking. There were tyres to change, spare parts to order and tons of tidying up. By lunchtime, he hadn't even got half of it done. Roary reversed into a corner of the workshop then called the other cars over. "We've got to help Big Chris," he whispered. "He's going to run out of time."
Cici flashed her headlights. "What will Big Christine say if there's no tree tonight?"

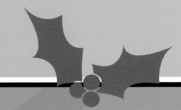

Big Chris skipped his lunchtime sarnie so that he could catch up time.
"I'm puffed out, Roary," he grumbled.
Ring! Ring!
Big Chris dug around his overalls, then flipped open his mobile.
"Hello! What Mum?" he gulped, looking at his watch. "You'll be here by five?"
The cars waited in silence until the mechanic hung up.
"Big Christine's caught an early train," he sighed.
"She's going to be here in an hour!"
Drifter revved his engine. "You can do it, Big Chris."
"There's still time if you go super-fast," added Maxi, although he didn't sound too convinced.

Big Chris cleaned, fixed and fitted as fast as his legs could carry him. By the time that he usually took a doughnut break, the poor mechanic was asleep on his broom.

"You're doing so well!" urged Roary. "Don't drop off now!"

Cici smiled enthusiastically. "There's still time to buy a Christmas tree."

Big Chris looked at Marsha's piece of paper then groaned. "No can do, Cici! I've still got to collect a stack of spare parts from the body shop."

The mechanic shook his head sadly and walked off to find Plugger. "Maybe Christmas isn't going to be so great after all."

ICY

When Big Chris and Plugger had gone, all the cars stared gloomily at each other.

"It's not fair," decided Drifter. "Big Chris was so excited about his mum coming."

"What's that?" asked Marsha, driving in on Zippee.

Roary looked cross. "You gave Big Chris so many jobs to do, he hasn't had time to get ready for Christmas!"

Marsha frowned.

"Why didn't you call me earlier?"

she asked. "We can't have Big Chris's Christmas spoiled!"

"Mamma Mia!" cried Maxi. "What are we waiting for?"

Roary's wheels spun. "We've only got a little while to put things right!"

While Big Chris was out, the team came up with a fabulous festive plan. Cici and Molecom were put in charge of finding a Christmas tree. They headed straight over to Silver Hatch Farm.

"'Course I'll help you," beamed Farmer Green, pointing to his pine forest. "I've got a bumper crop of trees this year." Molecom burrowed his way over to the fir trees then popped out of the mud.

"Which one shall we choose, Cici?" he asked.

The stunt car looked around then grinned.
"The biggest one, of course!"
Back in the workshop, everyone was
working as hard as they could. Maxi
polished the cars' bonnets, while Drifter
swept up the nuts and bolts.
"This way, Tin Top," shouted Roary, draping
tinsel all round the parking spaces.
Marsha grabbed her purse, then jumped
onto Zippee. She just had enough
time to dash to the shops.
"I'll pick up some presents, sticky tape
and wrapping paper," she announced.
"Radio me if Big Chris comes back."

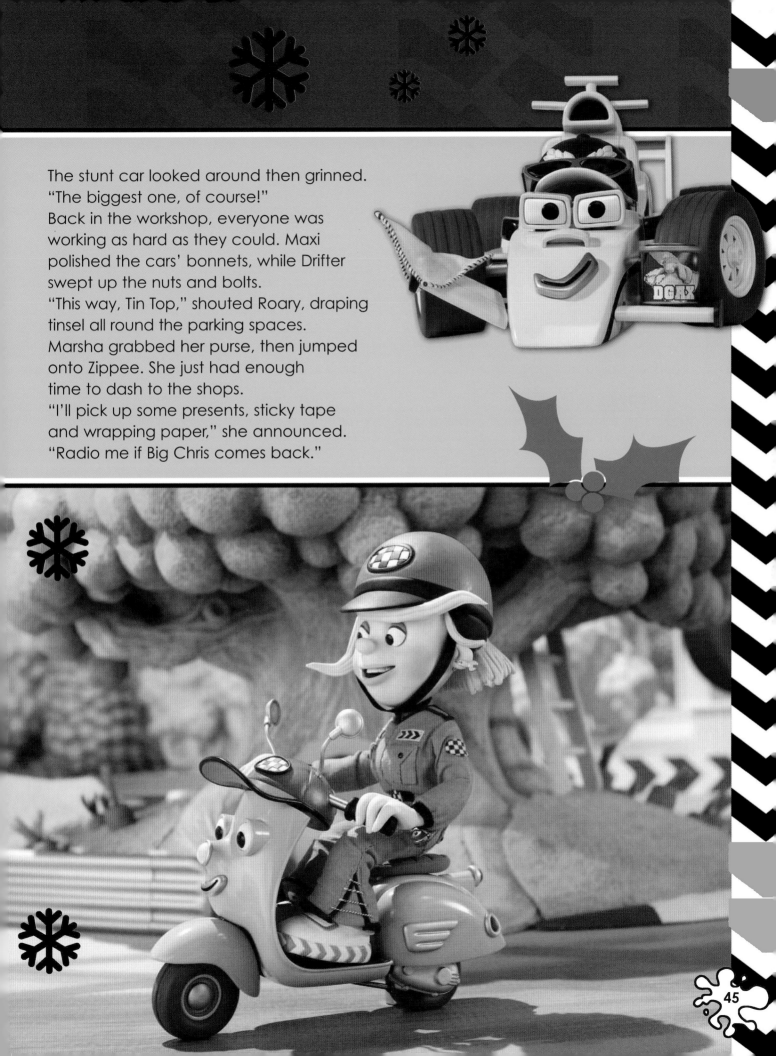

By the time Big Chris got back to Silver Hatch, it was dark. "What a day," he sighed, opening the workshop doors. "And I didn't even catch the shops."

Roary whizzed out to meet the mechanic. "Never mind, Big Chris. Your mum will understand."

"Understand what?" boomed a raspy voice. Big Chris and Roary both turned to find Big Christine standing behind them.

"Mum!" cried Big Chris. "I'm not quite ready, you see?"

"No, I don't see," frowned Big Christine, tucking her bag under her arm. "You look ready to me." The lady pointed to the lights glowing inside the workshop.

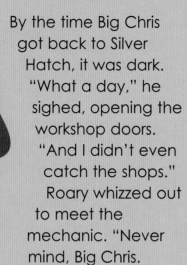

"Are you going to let me in, son? It's freezing out here!"

"Sorry, Mum," sighed Big Chris, flicking on the main workshop light. The mechanic did a double take – all the Silver Hatch team were waiting inside.
"Happy Christmas!" everyone cheered. "We thought we'd help with a job or two!" beamed Roary, feeling very proud of himself.
For the first time ever, Big Chris was speechless. He couldn't take his eyes off the sparkling Christmas tree and the stacks of presents.

ICY

"W-where did you get all that?" he finally stuttered. Marsha shook her head and smiled. "All you need to worry about is having a good Christmas!"
Big Christine grabbed herself a cracker, then offered the other end to her son.
"Well," she laughed. "What's my boy waiting for?"

47

"You beauties!" roared Big Chris a while later. "You really got me this time."
Roary grinned, then handed his friend a stocking full of gifts.
"Happy Christmas, Big Chris."
The mechanic took the stocking, then smiled. "Stop it, lad," he cooed. "I'm welling up now."

When Marsha started the carol singing, Big Chris nipped outside. He had a few surprises to hand out himself.
Over the weeks he'd been hiding little presents in Rusty – now was the perfect time to give them out.
"Jeeping jingle bells!" yelled the mechanic suddenly.
Everyone stopped singing.
Big Chris's eyes were wide.
"You lot had better follow me."

Roary gasped – Silver Hatch had been transformed into a winter wonderland! Rusty, the track and everything else was covered in a thick layer of white snow! Big Christine pulled her coat tightly around her. "Oooh, it's lovely!"

"Oh yes!" Cici giggled, as snowflakes tickled her windscreen wipers.

"Let's play!" shouted Maxi. He rolled up a snowball then threw it at Tin Top. Tin Top skidded to one side, letting the snowball land with a soft puff on Roary's bonnet.

"What do you think, Big Chris?" asked Roary.

"I think," said Big Chris, nodding his head, "that this is going to be the best Christmas ever!"

49

Car Challenge

There are lots of cars and other vehicles at Silver Hatch.
Can you find them all in the word grid below?

R	O	A	R	Y	D	O	A	R	T
H	Y	D	W	N	J	K	L	S	Q
L	S	R	R	H	J	Y	C	J	W
H	A	W	M	M	A	X	I	R	B
T	J	Q	X	N	M	G	C	H	G
F	D	Y	W	W	E	B	I	H	J
P	R	H	S	L	S	R	H	K	L
T	I	N	T	O	P	S	W	Q	O
G	F	N	L	A	W	R	O	Q	A
E	T	J	L	D	H	F	J	R	E
E	E	O	E	A	A	N	I	C	K
H	R	L	R	I	E	R	G	K	G
H	E	L	L	I	E	A	Q	R	T
N	R	I	F	B	C	V	N	M	Z
M	D	W	V	B	R	E	E	Z	E

ROARY	MAXI	CICI	DRIFTER	TIN TOP
JAMES	BREEZE	NICK	LOADA	HELLIE

50

Tool Hunt

Molecom's lost his tools again! Can you find all five of them scattered around Breeze's beach shack?

REFUEL

Cone Crazy

PC Pete thinks safety is very important. He's put up so many warning signs, barriers and cones that he can't even find a path back to Nick! Can you show him the way?

Start

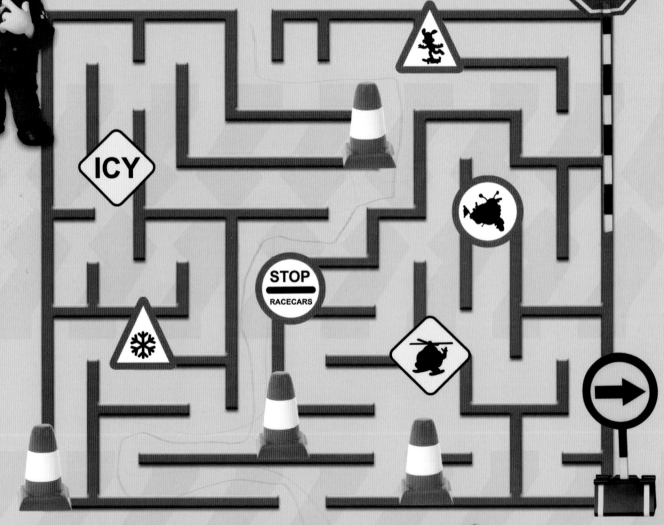

Finish

Find the Real Roary

Which one of these pictures of Roary below matches the real Roary shown here?

a

b

c

d

Picture [ ] is the same.

Spot the Differences

Roary is zooming around the track. But there are five differences in the picture on the right. Can you find them all?

Tin Top Tracing →

Trace over the lines to finish this picture of poor bashed-up
Tin Top, then colour him in – gently!

88

56

Where's James?

Mama Mia wants to go home but she can't find James!
Can you guide her down the right path to find him?

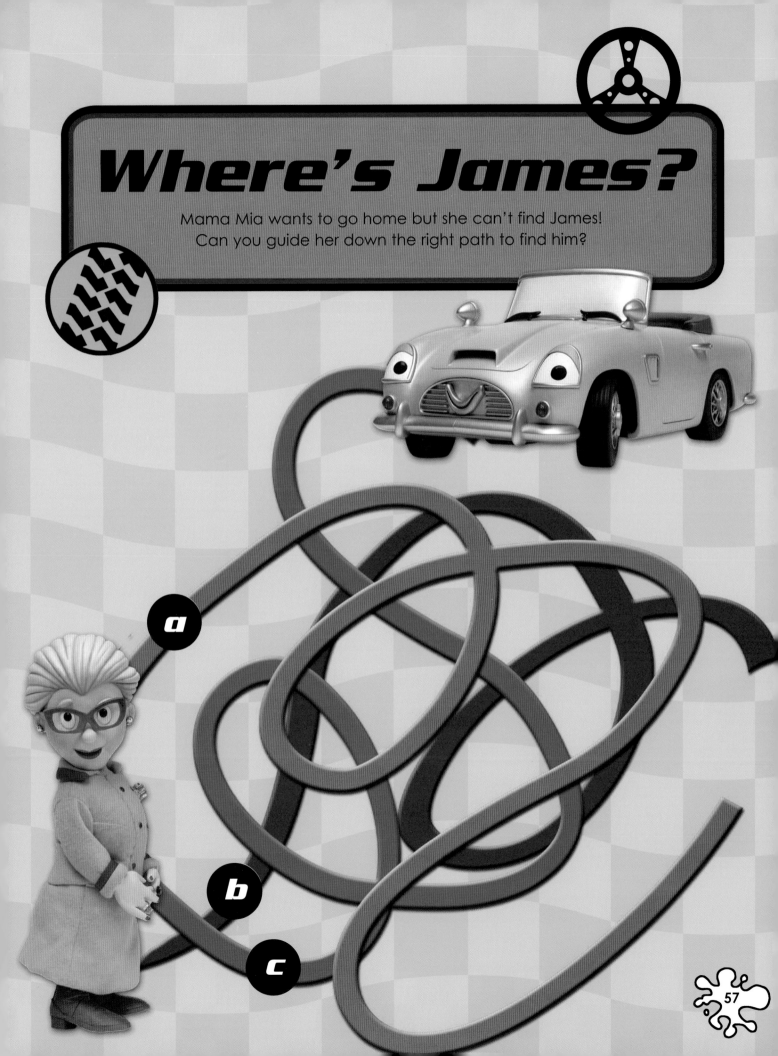

a

b

c

57

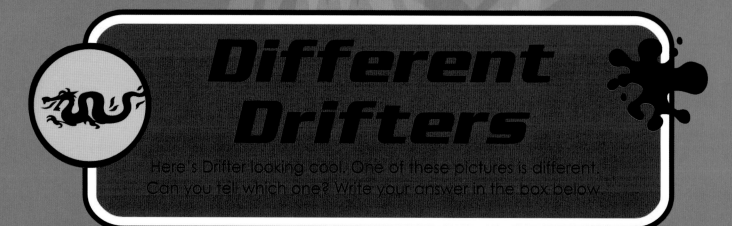

Different Drifters

Here's Drifter looking cool. One of these pictures is different.
Can you tell which one? Write your answer in the box below.

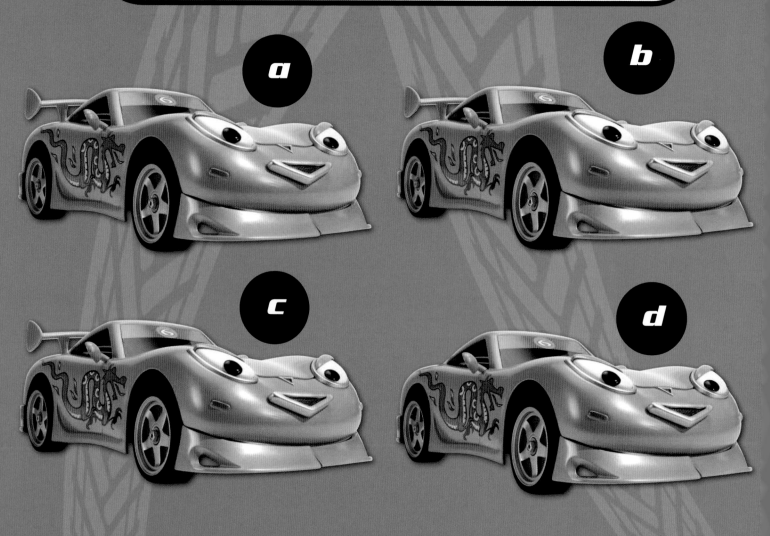

a

b

c

d

Picture ☐ is different from the others.

Answers

Page 8 **Welcome to Silver Hatch**
Pictures b, d and f are shown in the larger scene.

Page 22 **Puddle Paths**
Roary should follow path b.

Page 24 **Save the Carrots**

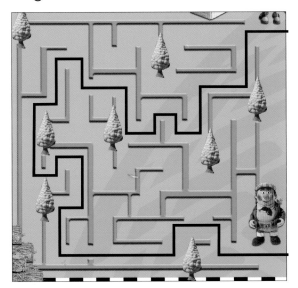

Page 26 **Ball Bounce**
Tin Top catches the beach ball.

Page 27 **Lost Post**

Page 28 **Match the Drivers**
A=2, B=3, C=1

Page 30 **Shadow Spotting**
A=Plugger, B=Drifter, C=Maxi, D=Cici

Page 31 **Jigsaw Jiggle**
Piece C is missing.

Page 33 **Tidying-up Time**
The present, letter and book aren't needed at the workshop.

Page 34 **Job Match**
A = Loada, B = Plugger, C = Hellie

Page 36 **Clever Chris**
There are 2 wrenches, 3 spanners and 4 screwdrivers.

Page 50 **Car Challenge**

R	O	A	R	Y	D	O	A	R	T
H	Y	D	W	N	J	K	L	S	Q
L	S	R	R	H	J	Y	C	J	W
H	A	W	M	M	A	X	I	R	B
T	J	Q	X	N	M	G	C	H	G
F	D	Y	W	W	E	B	I	H	J
P	R	H	S	L	S	R	H	K	L
T	I	N	T	O	P	S	W	Q	O
G	F	N	L	A	W	R	O	Q	A
E	T	J	L	D	H	F	J	R	E
E	E	O	E	A	A	N	I	C	K
H	R	L	R	I	E	R	G	K	G
H	E	L	L	I	E	A	Q	R	T
N	R	I	F	B	C	V	N	M	Z
M	D	W	V	B	R	E	E	Z	E

Answers

Page 51 **Tool Hunt**

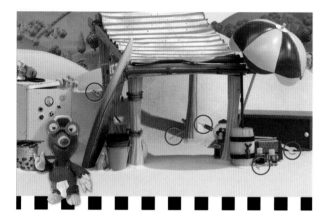

Page 54 **Spot the Differences**

Page 52 **Cone Crazy**

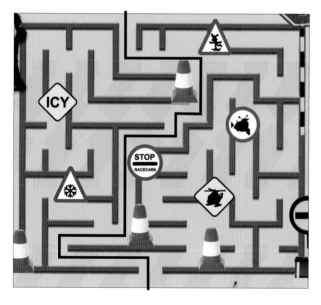

Page 57 **Where's James?**

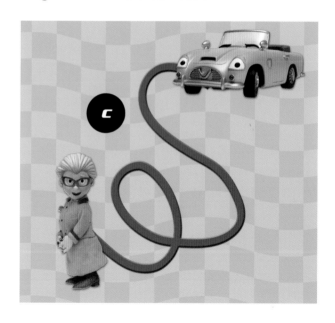

Page 53 **Find the Real Roary**
Picture b is the same.

Page 58 **Different Drifters**
Picture d is different from the others.

Check out our other great pre-school magazines...